BATMAN™
BATTLES
THE PENGUIN

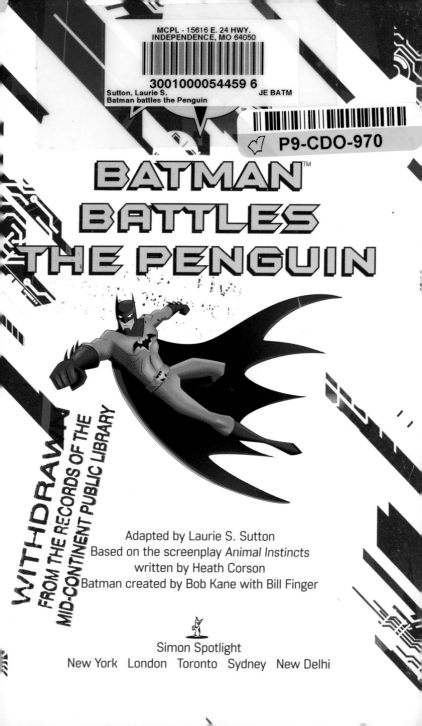

Adapted by Laurie S. Sutton
Based on the screenplay *Animal Instincts*
written by Heath Corson
Batman created by Bob Kane with Bill Finger

Simon Spotlight
New York London Toronto Sydney New Delhi

SIMON SPOTLIGHT
An imprint of Simon & Schuster Children's Publishing Division
1230 Avenue of the Americas, New York, New York 10020
This Simon Spotlight edition August 2016. All rights reserved, including the right of
reproduction in whole or in part in any form. SIMON SPOTLIGHT and colophon are
registered trademarks of Simon & Schuster, Inc. For information about special
discounts for bulk purchases, please contact Simon & Schuster Special
Sales at 1-866-506-1949 or business@simonandschuster.com.
Manufactured in the United States of America 0716 LAK
10 9 8 7 6 5 4 3 2 1
ISBN 978-1-4814-7855-7 (hc)
ISBN 978-1-4814-7854-0 (pbk)
ISBN 978-1-4814-7856-4 (eBook)

CHAPTER 1

Batman soared through the nighttime sky above Gotham City, using the glider mode of his newest Batsuit. A giant TV screen on the side of a building played the news. The Midas Heart—an asteroid with a solid gold core—would soon pass by Earth. But that wasn't on Batman's radar . . . yet. Tonight, he scanned the streets for trouble. It didn't take him long to find it.

Batman flew over S.T.A.R. Labs. Sensors in

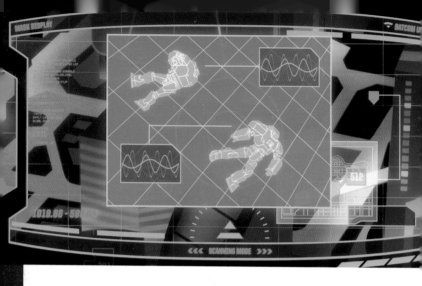

the eye lenses of his mask revealed that the guards were lying on the ground. Batman wasted no time and dived down toward the lab.

Inside, a robotic Cyber Wolf worked its way past all the security measures. Its belly opened and tentacles snaked out to grab a valuable piece of tech. Suddenly, a Batarang flew into the tentacles, keeping them from reeling in the prize.

"That doesn't belong to you," Batman said.

The robot's response was to punch a hole through the ceiling and escape! Batman chased the wolf across the rooftops of S.T.A.R. Labs and onto a major highway. The Cyber Wolf caused a traffic snarl that distracted the Dark Knight long enough for it to speed away.

Not far away, another Gotham City crime fighter battled a feline foe. Nightwing faced Cheetah in a jewelry store. Cheetah was just as fast as her namesake . . . and a very skilled opponent. In the middle of the fight, the floor under their feet started to rumble. Up burst Killer Croc!

"Finish the mission. I'll take care of him," Croc said to Cheetah.

Nightwing didn't have time to wonder what the villains' "mission" was. He was too busy

dodging Croc's fists. While Nightwing was distracted, Cheetah attacked him from behind and knocked him unconscious.

"Let's scram before Batman shows up," Killer Croc said.

Out of nowhere, The Flash arrived. "Leaving? But I just got here," the Scarlet Speedster quipped. He zipped around the villains at super speed.

Nightwing recovered and helped The Flash battle the two super-villains. But much to the heroes' surprise, Cheetah and Croc combined forces to escape.

At the Gotham National Bank, a giant gorilla was breaking into the vault. But this was no ordinary giant gorilla—it was Silverback! He had a bionic eye and a brilliant mind.

Just then a pair of green arrows halted Silverback in his tracks, and the Emerald Archer confronted the super-villain.

"Green Arrow!" Silverback exclaimed as he fired lasers at his foe.

The bank soon became a battleground. Silverback used the interior architecture as his personal jungle gym while Green Arrow used his special arrows to try and defeat the humongous gorilla. Suddenly, the shadow of a bat fell over Green Arrow!

"You're a sight for sore eyes, Bats," Green Arrow said, figuring that the bat shadow was none other than Batman. Then he heard a hideous screech. "Batman?"

"You have it backward," Silverback gloated. "Meet Man-Bat!"

The hideous winged villain swooped down and knocked Green Arrow into Silverback's grip.

"We are the Animilitia," Silverback declared proudly. "You will not stop us."

"Maybe not. But *he* will," Green Arrow replied, looking over the gorilla's shoulder. The real Batman had arrived!

Green Arrow and Batman teamed up to fight Silverback and Man-Bat. They were close to defeating the villains when a Cyber Tiger and a giant Cyber Bat arrived as backup—for the bad guys! Green Arrow and Batman did their best to try to stop them, but the villains escaped. What did all these powerful bad guys have in store for Gotham City?

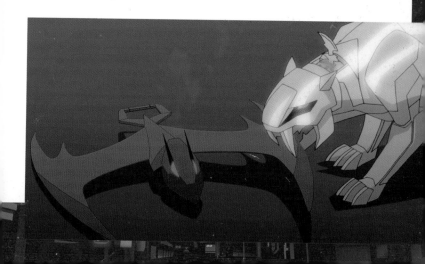

CHAPTER 2

Later, in the Batcave, Batman used his Batcomputer to analyze the night's crimes. Between Silverback and Man-Bat, Cheetah and Croc, and those Cyber Animals, he wondered if there was something bigger at play.

"You always say there's a pattern," Red Robin observed. "So, what's the pattern?"

Batman mapped out the Animilitia's crimes on a map of Gotham City. Eleven dots flashed on the

screen. They formed a circle around the Aviary Building—the city's newest, tallest building built by a wealthy investor named Oswald Cobblepot.

A few hours later, Bruce Wayne arrived at the high-society party for the grand opening of the Aviary Building. There, he met Oliver Queen, who secretly fought crime as Green Arrow. They listened as Oswald Cobblepot welcomed everyone.

"You were promised surprises tonight," said Cobblepot. "And here they are!"

Cobblepot introduced the latest in robotic designs from Bumbershoot Mechanics. Bruce and Oliver were surprised to see a Cyber Wolf, a Cyber Tiger, and a Cyber Bat appear on stage. They were the same robots that Batman and the other super heroes had fought. Cobblepot was up to something, but what? Then Dr. Kirk Langstrom, the engineer who designed the Cyber Animals, came on stage.

"He'll know what Cobblepot is planning. We need to talk to him," Bruce said. "But not here. Not dressed like this."

Oliver flicked a small tracking device. It flew through the air and attached itself to Langstrom's pants. Now they could keep tabs on him.

Back at the Batcave, Batman and Red Robin reviewed the clues again on the Batcomputer. Eleven crimes had been committed by the Animilitia in a ring around the Aviary Building. They were spaced out like the numbers on a clock, except there was one missing.

"The Gotham City Zoo," Batman observed. He had a hunch that one more crime was about to happen. Then the circle would be complete. "Alert the others."

There was work to be done.

CHAPTER 3

The super-villains made their way underground to the Gotham City Zoo.

"Complete the mission," said Silverback, commanding his team. Together, they broke in, ready to follow orders.

But the villains were not alone. Batman and his super hero comrades were already there!

"About time you guys got here," Green Arrow said. Then they all began to battle.

Batman went after Cheetah. Green Arrow took off after Killer Croc, and The Flash chased Silverback into the gorilla house. Nightwing and Red Robin decided to pursue Man-Bat.

Batman and Cheetah played a game of cat and mouse in the trees of the zoo's jungle habitat. From below, pumas and jaguars growled and roared.

"You dress as one of us, but secretly you fear your animal nature," Cheetah said as she perched on a branch above her nemesis. "You bury your animal instincts beneath layers of duty and order. Allow me to carve them out for you!"

Cheetah dropped down to meet Batman, but he jumped away from her raking claws. That's when she saw the blinking red light of a bat-shaped device on the branch. *BOOOOM!* Cheetah leaped out of the way just in time. Batman tossed another Batarang at her, and she caught it in her claws.

FAWOOOOOM! Just like that, the Batarang that Cheetah was holding erupted with a knockout energy pulse.

Not far away, Green Arrow tracked Killer Croc to the reptile house. He followed Croc's big footprints to the crocodile pond. One reptile there was not like the others.

"I can see you," Green Arrow said. "Even if I couldn't, man, could I *smell* you."

Killer Croc rose up out of the water. Green Arrow fired an arrow at the beast, but it crumpled against Croc's thick hide. The Emerald Archer loaded net arrows onto his bow and fired. One net wrapped around Killer Croc, but it didn't stop him. He tore right through it! Croc grabbed Green Arrow and wrapped up the super hero in the remains of his own net. Green Arrow's arms were bound together.

"Let's see you shoot now. Haw haw haw!" Killer Croc laughed.

Green Arrow may not have been able to use his hands, but he could still use his teeth. As the overconfident villain walked away, Green Arrow placed his bow in his mouth and took aim.

FWOOOSH! The villain turned around just as the hero fired. Knockout gas bloomed and Killer Croc breathed it in. He wobbled and fell unconscious—right on top of Green Arrow!

Over at the gorilla enclosure, The Flash looked for Silverback. But just when he found the ape, the speedster stepped into a snare! He was caught.

"I would say you are a worthy opponent, Flash," Silverback said. "But I hate to lie."

Silverback got away, leaving The Flash dangling above the ground.

The Flash was surrounded by the zoo's curious gorilla residents. *BOP! BOP!* They batted at him as if he were a toy.

"Well, this is embarrassing," The Flash said. "I'm the world's fastest man. I can't get beaten by a length of rope." Then a realization dawned on him. "It's just a length of rope!"

The Scarlet Speedster rubbed his free foot against the rope at super speed. The friction made it snap. The Flash was free! It didn't take him long to find Silverback. The Flash ran circles around the villain and smacked him with super speed punches until the giant gorilla fell down, defeated.

At the same time, Nightwing and Red Robin crept through the zoo's bat cavern looking for Man-Bat. They finally found him hanging upside down from the ceiling. Red Robin hurled a throwing disc at the beast. Man-Bat's loud screech sent all the bats in the cave swarming toward the two heroes.

"My bad," Red Robin admitted. Man-Bat grabbed Red Robin in his talons and flew out of the cavern with him.

Outside, in the zoo's central plaza, Batman, Green Arrow, and The Flash tied up the captured super-villains.

"I thought this plan was foolproof," Killer Croc complained.

"Correct. I've requested backup," Silverback replied.

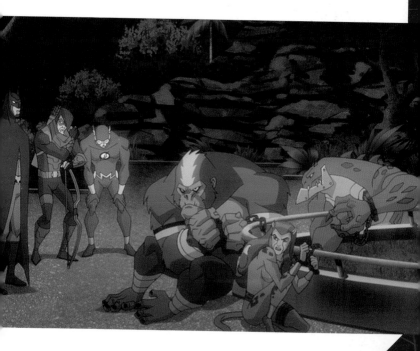

Screeeeeeee! Just then Man-Bat swooped overhead. He dropped Red Robin into the flamingo pond and circled around to rescue his comrades. He snapped their restraints just as Silverback declared, "Estimated arrival in three, two, one."

Suddenly, the trio of Cyber Animals leaped onto the scene. Silverback and Cheetah grabbed onto the Cyber Bat and were lifted into the sky. Man-Bat snatched Killer Croc and flew off. The villains had gotten away again—and the heroes were left to face the Cyber Wolf and Cyber Tiger!

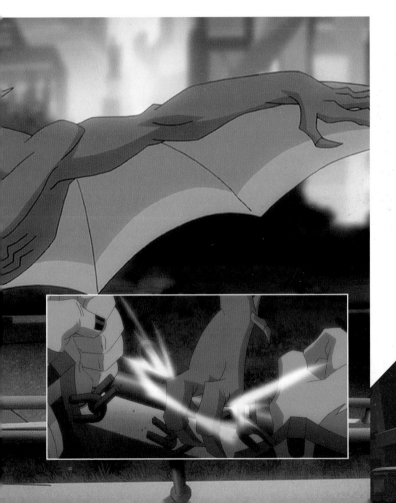

CHAPTER 4

"You want me? Come and get me," Batman challenged the Cyber Animals.

He held up a small remote-control device and the Batmobile roared toward him. He jumped in and peeled out. The Cyber Animals ran after him!

The Batmobile sped through the Gotham City streets. Red Robin and Green Arrow joined the chase on a Batcycle. Then the Cyber Bat returned and started firing its lasers at the Batmobile.

Green Arrow disabled the Cyber Bat with an explosive arrow. Batman made sharp turns in the Batmobile and used a construction site like an obstacle course before dropping a load of steel beams onto the Cyber Wolf. Nightwing finished the robot off with a super-electric charge from his eskrima sticks. The Cyber Tiger met its match when The Flash steered it toward a concrete wall. The Flash stopped, but the robot crashed into the wall at maximum speed.

The three disabled Cyber Animals were taken to the Batcave so Batman and the others could analyze the robots' impressive engineering. It was clear the Cyber Animals' designer, Dr. Langstrom, was a genius.

But Batman wondered why Cobblepot used the Animilitia and the Cyber Animals to commit robberies in the first place. Even stranger, nothing was stolen at the bank, the jewelry store, or the zoo. Perhaps the villains weren't there to take anything—they were there to *leave* something. But what?

It was time to question Dr. Langstrom. The Dark Knight activated Langstrom's tracking device and a red dot blinked on a map of Gotham City. He was at Bumbershoot Mechanics.

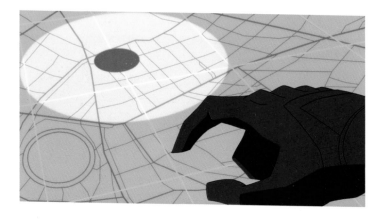

Batman and his allies headed for that location just as Cobblepot met with his Animilitia allies. Cobblepot called himself the Penguin now. Since the Animilitia had visited the zoo, the last piece of his plan was in place . . . and just in the nick of time. The Midas Heart asteroid would soon be close to Earth. It was the moment the Penguin had been waiting for.

Suddenly, an arrow burst through the window of Bumbershoot Mechanics headquarters and skewered the Penguin's top hat. Another arrow deployed a net and pinned him to the wall. It was Green Arrow! Silverback and Cheetah took off after him.

A moment later, an explosion blasted a hole in the ceiling, and Batman and Nightwing dropped through it to confront Man-Bat and Killer Croc. Batman grappled with Man-Bat and they crashed through the window. The Penguin freed himself as Nightwing and Croc fought, and he used his electrified umbrella to knock Nightwing unconscious. He ordered Croc to toss Nightwing out of the smashed window.

The Flash saw his falling comrade and ran straight up the side of the building to catch him.

"I can't believe you saved me," Nightwing said.

"Me too. I've never run up a building before," The Flash admitted.

Above them, Batman struggled with Man-Bat. But as he fought, the Dark Knight noticed a bat-shaped tracking device attached to the creature's pant leg.

"Langstrom?" Batman realized. He slapped a sonic scrambler onto Man-Bat's head. The pulse knocked out the creature. It was time to get some answers.

CHAPTER 5

Back in the Batcave, Batman analyzed Man-Bat's blood. He concluded that the creature was Dr. Langstrom, transformed due to an experiment gone wrong, and also under the Penguin's control! Batman synthesized an antidote and restored Langstrom to human form, but it was only temporary. Still, Dr. Langstrom was grateful and agreed to help Batman.

Langstrom explained the mechanics of the

Cyber Animals. With his help, the heroes repaired and reassembled the robots to learn more about them. But Langstrom couldn't tell the super heroes much about the Penguin's plan. He only knew about the role the Cyber Animals would play.

Suddenly, the clues connected for Batman! He realized that the Animilitia had left receivers at each of the fake robbery sites. Together, these receivers would form a force field around the Aviary Building. But why would the Penguin need a force field?

"The Midas Heart!" Batman realized. "The Penguin is going to crash the asteroid into Gotham City. He's going to use the Cyber Animals to sort through the rubble and retrieve the gold at the center of it." The rest of Gotham City would be wiped out from the asteroid, and the Penguin—along with his Animilitia—would survive, with all the riches they could ever want!

Before they left to stop the Penguin, Batman and his team of super heroes locked Dr. Langstrom back in his chamber. The antidote wore off, and with a shriek, Dr. Langstrom transformed back into the ferocious creature.

In the penthouse of the Aviary Building, the Penguin and the Animilitia set the master plan into motion. The force field deployed around the building and a tractor beam shot into the sky. It grabbed the Midas Heart asteroid and pulled it from orbit—right toward Gotham City!

But Batman had his own plan. He arrived at the base of the force field wearing an unusual Batsuit. Police Commissioner Gordon and the Gotham City Police Department (G.C.P.D.) had already thrown explosives at the shield and could not penetrate it. Now it was Batman's turn to try.

Batman powered up the suit and walked right through the force field! The Penguin was

astonished. He ordered his Cyber Animals to take out his foe. An army of Cyber Wolves, Cyber Tigers, and Cyber Bats swarmed out onto the street. Batman stared down the threat and spoke a single command.

"Ace, come."

A Cyber Wolf leaped out of the pack and transformed into a motorcycle. Batman had hacked the robot to follow his commands—not the Penguin's! He jumped onto the vehicle and zoomed down the street. The horde of Cyber Animals took off after the Dark Knight.

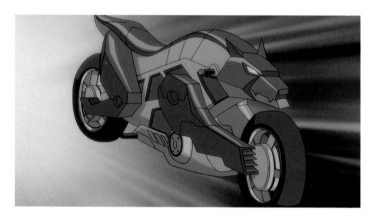

Meanwhile, The Flash used his super speed to get past the force field too. Once he was inside, he raced to take out a receiver that was planted at one of the fake robbery sites. If he destroyed just one receiver, the whole force field would fail.

Cyber Tigers chased The Flash all the way to the Gotham National Bank. They used their robotic tails to snag his legs and his body. The Flash was almost stopped in his tracks. But then a hacked Cyber Tiger attacked the other robots! The Flash was able to find the Penguin's receiver in the bank vault—right where Silverback had planted it.

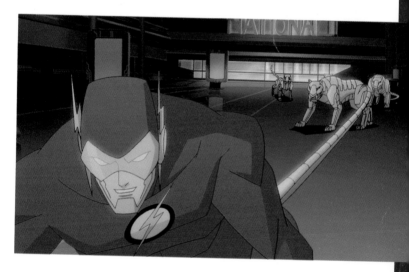

"Here, boy!" The Flash called to the friendly Cyber Tiger. The robot crushed the receiver in its jaws. It worked! The link to the force field failed. The force field around the Aviary Building deactivated.

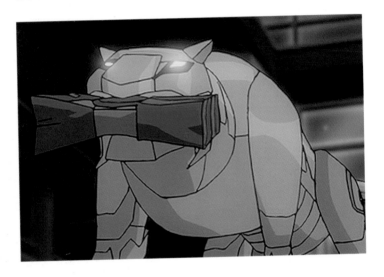

In the penthouse, the Penguin's control console went out. But the tractor beam that was pulling the giant asteroid down toward Gotham City was still operational. The asteroid was coming closer and closer, but there wasn't a force field to protect the Penguin anymore! Lucky for him, he had a backup plan. He jumped into an escape pod and launched into the sky, abandoning his Animilitia allies—and everyone else in Gotham City—to their fate.

With the force field down, Red Robin was able

to start a special upload from the Batcomputer in the Batcave. But behind him, Man-Bat broke out of his cell and screeched like a wild animal.

"Dr. Langstrom, please. I know you can hear me. We're trying to help you," Red Robin pleaded.

Man-Bat shook his head as if trying to clear his mind. Then he flapped his wings and took off, but not before Red Robin jumped onto his back and hung on for dear life! Behind them, the upload reached completion.

Suddenly, the Cyber Animals chasing Batman

stopped in their tracks. Red Robin's upload contained a computer virus, and it worked! Batman called Red Robin on the radio to congratulate him on a successful upload, but the young crime fighter was busy trying to hold on to Man-Bat and appeal to the mind trapped inside the monster.

"Dr. Langstrom, please! Your body has changed, but not your mind. Concentrate," Red Robin urged.

Man-Bat's face contorted and then his eyes

widened as if waking up from a nightmare. He still looked like Man-Bat, but Dr. Langstrom was back!

"I knew you could do it! Let's get to the others," Red Robin said.

Meanwhile, in the Aviary Building, Batman, Nightwing, Green Arrow, and The Flash confronted the Animilitia. The hacked Cyber Tiger and Cyber Wolf stood beside the super heroes. Batman gave a simple order to the robots.

"Take them."

The Cyber Beasts leaped toward the Animilitia. *BONK! BAM! THUMP!* The robots defeated the super-villains.

"So, the bad guys are down, but what about the giant flaming rock?" Green Arrow said as the heroes examined the Penguin's destroyed control console.

The super heroes may have defeated the Penguin and his Animilitia, but they still had to save Gotham City!

CHAPTER 6

Luckily, Batman knew just how to save the city. He sent Nightwing and The Flash to find electronic parts. Meanwhile, he instructed Green Arrow to find a new power source for the control console. The Emerald Archer plugged a thick power cable into the cybernetic systems of the unconscious Silverback, who, as it turns out, was really a cyborg all along.

A short time later, Nightwing finished building

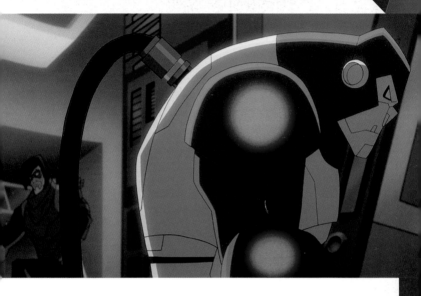

a device made out of the electronic parts. But he still had to get it up to the tractor beam antenna on the roof of the Aviary Building so they could guide the asteroid away.

"Maybe we can help," Red Robin said as he flew in on the back of Man-Bat.

But Batman was already on the roof rewiring the antenna. The descending asteroid was huge in the sky above him. Over his radio, Batman instructed The Flash to collect the remaining force field receivers and place them at the edges of Gotham City.

The Scarlet Speedster raced to the Gotham City Zoo and to all the other sites where the Animilitia had placed receivers. Then he repositioned them in a circle around the city.

Back at the Aviary Building, Batman and Man-Bat were ready to begin the final phase of Batman's plan, but it meant that Man-Bat had to fly into the tractor beam. It was the only way that Nightwing's device could focus the signal. Man-Bat took it and leaped upward.

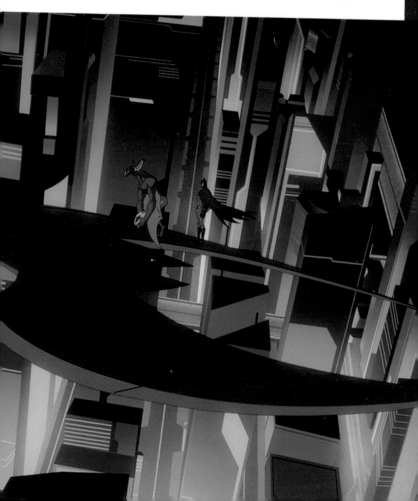

The massive asteroid streaked toward the city in a ball of flame. Green Arrow stood ready at the controls to the tractor beam. He waited for the command from Batman to shoot the Midas Heart back into space. But Batman had a different plan. He wanted Green Arrow to pull the asteroid into Gotham City.

"We can't reverse the asteroid's trajectory," Batman said, "but I've rewired the force field and The Flash has moved the receivers. If my calculations are correct, we should be safe."

"And if they aren't?" Green Arrow observed.

"They are. *Now!*" Batman commanded.

Green Arrow pressed the control button. It activated the device in Man-Bat's hands as he stood in the line of the tractor beam. The beam changed color and a new force field began to form over Gotham City. But would it be strong enough? Citizens and super heroes held their breath.

BAAAWHAAAAAAAM! The asteroid exploded against the shield. Chunks of debris landed harmlessly in the Gotham River. Gotham City was safe!

Inside the tractor beam, Man-Bat screeched for the last time. His wings started to shrink. His claws and talons disappeared. He transformed back to human form. Then the tractor beam and force field faded away, and Dr. Langstrom fell!

Batman flew in and rescued him just in time.

Later, Dr. Langstrom woke up on a couch in the Aviary Building penthouse. Batman told him that a power surge through the tractor beam had burned out all traces of Man-Bat in Langstrom's DNA.

"Thank you, Batman. Thank you for giving me my life back," Langstrom said.

Meanwhile, the Animilitia were headed for a life in prison. The super-villains were loaded into police transport trucks as Batman and his comrades watched from a nearby roof.

"Never a dull moment in Gotham City. It's just a shame that the Penguin got away," Green Arrow observed.

The heroes nodded in agreement, and then they said good-bye. Until next time, anyway. . . .

Far away, the Penguin stepped out of his damaged escape pod. He had wanted to flee

to the Greek Isles, but instead he landed in Antarctica. It was not the destination he had programmed. Then he saw a green arrow stuck in an exterior control panel. It had obviously tampered with his plan.

Suddenly, a group of penguins appeared in the fog and waddled toward the Penguin. They surrounded him as if he were a part of their flock.

"No! No! Stay away! Leave me alone! Have you no sense of personal space?" the Penguin

protested. But the birds continued to gather.

The Penguin was surrounded.

"I'll get you, Batman!" the Penguin vowed.